PIRATES
DON'T SAY
PLEASE!

PIRATES
DON'T SAY
PLEASE!

By Laurie Lazzaro Knowlton
Illustrated by Adrian Tans

PELICAN PUBLISHING COMPANY
Gretna 2012

For J. C.
Also for Pirate Billy Nelson and his scallywag mates, Maggie and Tom.

Copyright © 2012
By Laurie Lazzaro Knowlton

Illustrations copyright © 2012
By Adrian Tans

The word "Pelican" and the depiction of a pelican are
trademarks of Pelican Publishing Company, Inc., and are
registered in the U.S. Patent and Trademark Office.

Library of Congress Cataloging-in-Publication Data

Knowlton, Laurie Lazzaro.
  Pirates don't say please! / by Laurie Lazzaro Knowlton ; illustrated by Adrian Tans.
    p. cm.
  Summary: When Billy uses pirate manners, Mom sends the scallywag to the brig until her polite son returns.
  ISBN 978-1-58980-982-6 (hc : alk. paper) [1. Etiquette--Fiction. 2. Pirates--Fiction. 3. Imagination--Fiction.] I. Tans, Adrian, ill. II. Title. III. Title: Pirates do not say please!
  PZ7.K7685Pi 2012
  [E]--dc23
                    2011047418

Printed in Singapore
Published by Pelican Publishing Company, Inc.
1000 Burmaster Street, Gretna, Louisiana 70053

PIRATES DON'T SAY PLEASE!

"Wash your hands for lunch!" said Mom.
"Pirates don't wash their hands," declared Pirate Billy Nelson.
"Wash their hands," repeated Parrot.
"I didn't invite pirates for lunch," said Mom.
"Back away from me bounty, poppet," cried Pirate Billy Nelson, "and I'll spare your life!"
"Spare your life!" said Parrot.

"Leave your parrot, your cutlass, and your pirate ways at the door," replied Mom, "or it's off to the brig with you."

"Prepare to be plundered," said Billy Nelson. He swooped in and grabbed a chicken leg.

"Plundered!" cried Parrot.

"To the brig, you scallywag," said Mom. "You'll be set free when you return my polite son."

"Arrrrgh!" said Billy Nelson. "Thar's not a prison can hold the likes of Pirate Billy Nelson. I'll be sailing the high seas before you can sing, 'Yo, ho, ho, and a bottle of scum!'"

"Yo, ho, ho!" sang Parrot.

"Off with you!" said Mom.

Billy Nelson sat in his room. His parrot paced back and forth.

Billy pulled out his spyglass. He searched the horizon from his prison. "We're in luck, Parrot. Thar's Elephant sailing a sloop."

"Sailing, sailing!" sang Parrot.

"Ahoy, me hearty!" called Pirate Billy Nelson. "Take pity on a man doomed to a dungeon. Set me free and I'll sail you to my buried treasure!"

"Climb aboard, Mate." Elephant extended his trunk. "Well?"

"Well what?" asked Pirate Billy Nelson.

"You didn't say thank you," replied Elephant.

"Pirates don't say thank you," declared Billy.

"Don't say thank you?" squawked Parrot.

"Treasure or not, you won't be sailing with me," said Elephant.

"Arrrrgh!" growled Billy Nelson. "I've been marooned. My legs are growing roots. I need the sea!"

"Need the sea!" echoed Parrot.

"Aye, Matey," said Pirate Billy Nelson. "I be no lily-livered landlubber!"

"Landlubber!" squawked Parrot. He flew to a tree.

Pirate Billy Nelson followed Parrot through a jungle to a busy port.

He pulled out his spyglass. "We're in luck, Parrot. Thar's merchant ships aplenty, waiting for a fine seaman like me-self."

"Merchant ships aplenty!" crooned Parrot.

"This looks like a mighty grand ship," said Billy. "I'll be sailing this gal to sea."

"Excuse me, sir," said the ship's captain. "You must say, 'Permission to board, please.'"

"Pirates don't say please!" replied Pirate Billy Nelson.

"Pirate?" asked Captain. "I'll not have a no-manners, scurvy pirate on my ship!"

"Arrrrgh!" said Pirate Billy Nelson. "Who'd want to sail with the lily-livered likes of you, Captain?"

"Lily-livered," screeched Parrot.

Billy pulled out his spyglass. "We're in luck, Parrot! Thar's a gem of a ship." While no one was looking, Pirate Billy Nelson stole on board, hoisted the anchor, and set sail.

Pirate Billy Nelson sailed past the sunset, beyond the North Star, to the sunrise on the leeward side of Jamaica, singing, "Sixteen men on a pirate's quest. Yo, ho, ho, and a bottle of scum!"

He dropped anchor and rowed his dinghy to shore.

He followed his treasure map: five paces to the double palm, twelve paces over the rocky river, three paces to the left of the cave, seven paces toward the skull stone, and *X* marks the spot.

Pirate Billy Nelson dug deep, deep, deep until . . . "My hidden booty!"

"Booty! Booty!" chanted Parrot.

Pirate Billy Nelson juggled the coins. He danced a jig. He chanted. He rolled in his treasure.

Finally, he fell asleep wearing jewels and a crown.

Pirate Billy Nelson awoke to his stomach grumbling. "Not a tavern for miles and miles. Arrrrgh! What's a pirate to do?"

"To do? To do?" asked Parrot.

From somewhere far, far away, Billy heard a sweet mother's song. He smelled the deliciousness of a dinner fit for a prince.

Pirate Billy Nelson knew just what to do.

"Dear Queen, your prince
has arrived with hands washed.
Many thanks for the banquet.
May the feast begin, please."
"Please?" asked Parrot.
"Silly Parrot," replied Billy.
"A prince always says please."